WAG

TO THE RESCUE

RAYMOND PAUL BOYD

To order additional copies of this book, contact:
Xlibris
844-714-8691
www.Xlibris.com
Orders@Xlibris.com

ISBN: 978-1-6641-2308-3 (sc)
ISBN: 978-1-6641-2307-6 (e)

Print information available on the last page

Rev. date: 09/26/2020

Raymond Paul Boyd

Published Titles

The Alpha Dracula
The Presidents Wife
It's Who You Know
The Log Cabin
The Shadow of Paradise
E-mail to Heaven
The Judgement of Sarah Solomon
Condemnation
Laraine Day FBI
Puppy in the White House

PROLOGUE

It's presume by the teaching of organized religion that immediate after death, the soul, depending whether or not the inhabitant has lived according to the dictates of their religion, shall enter into the kingdom of God. Those who defy the teaching have condemned their soul to an eternity of damnation. In this narrative, we see that Wag's short time on earth as protector is intertwined with a small number of the human race, of which the majority sincerely love an assortment of God's lesser creatures.

DEDICATION

To my wife, Gloria, September 10, 1934–August 18, 2000.
As always, her presence is felt the moment I begin to
formulate a story. She has been my spiritual cowriter.

To Be or Not to Be?

I nervously awaited the answer I had wished that after four years of earth time, Bow-Wow would grant my return to earth. As comforter, I was certain by explaining that I had learned my lesson, Bow-Wow would give me another chance. I had wished to speak with him alone. I had feared Bow-Wow would refuse my request, and I would be embarrassed, as it was customary that when speaking to the all-knowing Bow-Wow, all in the kingdom be present. But as expected, there was no exception to the rule. Therefore, once again, I stood on the stage of the great hall. I nervously began to wag my tail as countless eyes stared at me, wondering what I was going to say. Now that I was standing face to face with Bow-Wow, I, too, was wondering.

I therefore decided to concentrate on the magically changing size of the great hall to make room for all in the animal kingdom. The entrance was made from the great oak tree in shape of an arch, the walls were trees of ivory, and perched on their branches were every manner of birds. The ceiling was made of pink cotton candy, the floor was golden-yellow straw. Many of the visitors ate their fill of the straw, which grew back as it was eaten. The singing birds stopped when Bow-Wow entered and raised his right paw. The great hall no longer increased in size as all in the kingdom had arrived. His coat of brown glistened like snow. Bow-Wow was twice the size of an ordinary shepherd. His large gray eyes seemed to possess wisdom and compassion. He then spoke in a normal voice, as it wasn't necessary to speak loud, as all in our kingdom could hear. "No matter the distance, sisters and brothers, we are here in appeal from Brother Wag."

He meant that I was to speak. I said with humility, "Sir, I want my job back."

Bow-Wow, as always, was direct. He replied, "Wag, I'm certain with the approval of all here, I grant your request, but not as comforter. If you accept, you shall return as a protector."

I was completely taken by surprised. I also knew Bow-Wow's offer was not debatable. Bow-Wow was aware that I would accept state the terms of returning back to earth. I was to have *no memory* of our heavenly animal kingdom. Only my name. "Do you accept?"

"Yes," I replied.

There was a thunder of applause, and the trumpets of the elephants was heard above all. Now the story I shall tell after I had completed my mission and recalled my memory after I had returned to the animal kingdom.

Kitty Cat, Kitty Cat, Kitty Cat

I was standing next to a tree. A buzzard was looking down at me, and there was a sound of babies crying in the buzzard's nest.

"What do you have in there?" I asked.

"My dinner," he replied. "After I go, get some salt. I shall return and have my dinner." Flapping his large black wings, he flew away.

I knew I had to act quickly, but the nest was around fifty feet high. I looked at my four paws and saw that I could climb up the trees. I then proceeded to embed my front claws into the tree when suddenly I saw about ten feet above me a fifteen-foot-long snake moving up to the sound of the crying. I was not certain what happened, but it happened so fast. I took hold of the end of the snake with my teeth firmly and flung him to the ground. I then proceed to the nest. I looked into the pail where the crying came from. To my surprise, inside were three kitten. They were about four weeks old.

I quickly took hold of the pail's handle with my mouth as I heard from a distance the flapping of the wings of the vulture with my super hearing. I began to run, but I got tired and took a moment to rest. Suddenly the clouds darken. As I looked, I saw the buzzard diving down; at that same instant, a bolt of lightning struck the path of the vulture. I knew that I must find shelter as the storm turned into a hurricane. I was fortunate I found a vacant house. I believed the mother and the father, who had been in search of their babies, didn't survive the storm. This I learned after I returned to the kingdom.

VACANT

Now, I had to find milk for the three kittens. I was also in need of food. Luck was with me; I decided to go in search of food when I saw a grocery store that had been ravished by the storm. The roof has been blown off. I helped myself to a quart of milk and two pounds of steak.

Two months later, I still remained with my adopted family. I had named them Kitty Cat 1, Kitty Cat 2, and Kitty Cat 3. In all that time, we were not intruded upon. But I couldn't help but feel we were not alone. I therefore thought it best to move elsewhere. Having drunk their milk. It's now time for their nap. I told them I would return soon.

Walking down the street, I was not paying attention to my surroundings, feeling proud of myself for all I had done for the three kittens. Had I not been so absorbed in self-pride, I could had prevented what happened next.

MILK

MILK

I saw one of two men. One was holding a long pole, and at the end of it was a noose made of wire. To my surprise, they slipped it over my neck. I knew it was useless to resist. The other man opened the rear doors of a van with words on the side panel that spelled Animal Control. I thought after they had taken me to the animal shelter, I would make my escape. Once again, I was taken by surprised as I heard one of the men say, "This Jack Russel looks great. He will fetch a good price." The pun caused both to laugh.

Their job was to take me to the animal shelter, but after twenty minutes, they stopped outside the city in front of a garage. A man was standing in front of it. As I was taken out, I heard the man say, "Is that all you have?" Then they haggled over a price for me. They shook hands, and the two drove away. I was taken inside and put into a wire cage next to two others.

ANIMAL
CONTROL

"Get some rest," one of them said to me.

"Why is that?" I asked.

"Because in two days, you will be put into a pit with one of us and fight for your life."

"And what are your names, may I ask?"

"We don't wish to tell you as one of us will have to fight with you to the death."

Ignoring what he believed to be a fact, I asked if they had thought to get away. They both laughed. "Did I say something funny?"

"Well, yes. The fact you have been here in the space of minutes and you are talking of escaping."

"I am surprised that both of you are pit bulls, and I would think you wouldn't give up, is that right?"

The other one, the smaller of the two who had remained wordless, asked, "Do you have a way out of here?"

"Yes," I replied with assurance. When it was good and dark and all was still, I sat patiently. I worried about Kitty Cat 1, Kitty Cat 2, and Kitty Cat 3, that hunger would cause them to leave the safety of the house.

I had saw that my fellow prisoner had bites that were infected. I believed once free, they could be made well. At 2:00 a.m., all was still, and I then proceeded to affect our escape. The two pit bulls were fast asleep as I stiffened my tail and pushed it between the wire cage and lifted the latch to freedom.

Luck was with us as the door had been left unlocked. Also our lives were saved as we were about ten feet from the barn when a bolt of lightning struck it. As a result, the barn caught on fire. I was about to suggest that we three stay together, but to my surprise, they began to run with purpose into an open door of light. There, standing in the door, was a glowing form of a large German shepherd. He beckoned the two pit bulls to enter. They did so. I watched in amazement at that time. I was unware that it was Bow-Wow. I stood motionless, but the sound of the sirens from the firetrucks snapped me back to reality, and suddenly, I was overcome with a feeling of danger. I knew the three kittens were in need of my help.

When Do We Eat?

The question was ask of Patch, the leader of a pack of rats. Speaking of the kittens, they were huddled together with a rope around their necks, mewing softly in fear. The question had been asked by Short Tail. “When they are fat enough to eat.” Patch’s word was law. He called the other rats his mob. Long Tail was second in charge. He secretively believed he should be the leader—after all, he had the longest tail, but for the fact Patch wore a suit of armor made from an empty can of beans and he and Short Tail’s suit of armor was made from an empty box of corn flakes and rice crisps.

“How long will it take?” Long Tail ask timidly.
“We must get milk and sardines.”
“May I say with due respect, sir, they look good enough to eat. Don’t you think?”
“Stupid, can’t you see it? Their bodies are covered with hair.”
“Then how about feeding them mice? We have plenty of them.”
“OK.”
“Do we have enough?” Short Tail asked.

Patch stood up on his hind legs, looming twice the size of all the other rats. Irritated that he was being questioned, he spoke in a loud voice, “Our sisters can produce an abundance of mice.” Patch’s demeanor caused the other rats to shake in fear as Patch walked to another room. There he had a store of cheese.

Short Tail spoke to Long Tail, “Why is he wearing a patch?”

“He wears it because it makes him look tough. If he didn’t have that armor on, I could beat him up,” said Long Tail.

“Well, maybe the two of us can,” Short Tail said with certainty.

“Let’s go and get some cheese, said Long Tail.

BEANS

Kitty Cat 1 said to his brothers, “Let us run away from here before the rats come back.”

“How can we get out of here?” asked Kitty Cat 2. “The door is locked.

“The window is opened a couple of inches. That’s enough for us to squeeze through,” said Kitty Cat 1. “Once we are outside, we can look for Wag. But for our safety, we must find a place to hide until morning.”

“That’s a good idea. Do you know the best place to go?” asked Kitty Cat 3.

“I know a place to hide. So let’s run as fast as we can from here until we find a big tree. We can then climb up and sleep, and at daylight, we can see from above when Wag returns.”

Now I was hiding not far from the burning barn. The police were also there. I was happy to see they had found where many dogs had been buried due to their injuries in fights. Several men were arrested. I thought it wise to rest until daylight and find my way back.

Of course, I hadn't known at the time that Patch and his mob of several hundred rats were out in search of the three kittens. Their hunt backfired as many of them became food for a dozen tomcats. Patch's suit of armor didn't save him.

BEANS

I somehow found my way back to the house where I had hope to find the kittens. A short distance before I arrived at the house, I saw a fire truck followed by a white van with letters that spelled Animal Control. I quickly ran under a park car. A few minutes later, I realized the meaning of what I had seen. It's now that I'm back in the animal kingdom that I learned what had happen to the kittens. They were unable to climb down. A passerby heard their cries and called 911. I was brokenhearted to find the room empty. I blamed myself for whatever misfortune that may have befell them.

J912
AN
CO

Oh, what to do? All of a sudden, I had a great idea. I would track their scent. A minute later, as I sniffed in vain to pick up the scent of Kitty Cat 1 or Kitty Cat 2 or 3, I sniffed the scent of ten or twelve older cats and many rats. I had determined, as I walked away, that a feeding frenzy had taken place. I was convinced that the three kittens weren't involved. I now had another thought as I recalled that I had seen the truck that captured stray animals. Just like a flash, I knew what I should do, and that was to go where the truck had gone. An hour later, I found the place. The constant barking of several dogs I heard from two miles away led me to my destination.

As I stood by the truck, I easily detected the scent of the kittens. I guessed they were locked inside a cage. Now I had to figure out how I was going to get myself in and the kittens out. As a good idea wasn't forthcoming, I thought it best to hide until I got an idea.

I was a block away in a wooded area when a thought came to me at midnight, and it was easy. All I had to do was dig under the fence that encircled the two building. I was able to get inside in less than two minutes, and I was taken by surprise when I saw the three kittens.

As I looked in the cage, it was plain to see they were being well taken care of, having been bathe and fed. Pink ribbons were tied loosely around their necks, and they were cuddled together, no doubt in a dream state of sleep. I hadn't thought in advance what I was going to do after I gotten them out. As I pondered the questions, my thoughts were interrupted by the bulldog in the next cage, asking if was not going to open the cage of the kittens. Then I should let him and the other out. Before I could respond, the others began to bark in agreement. In a whisper, I cautioned them to be quiet as I unlocked the cage of the bulldog. Freed of his confinement, he began to set free the others. But he as well as I were at a loss when most of others refused to leave their confinement. Although the three kittens remained peaceful asleep, I decided they, too, should remain. My instinct was that this was the best place for them. At the time, I hadn't known that the pink ribbons around their necks meant they had been adopted by a good family that lived on a farm.

I led only ten dogs and six cats that left their cages. The bull dog led the way out through the kitchen as opposed to the way I had entered so we could eat our fill before our escape. Two days later, the six cats returned to the shelter as they found eating mice and rats disgusting.

All's Well that Ends Well

Six of the ten dogs were German shepherds under the age of two. They were taken in by police departments in two nearby cities. The other four and three pit bulls and a bulldog had been taken in by four families. I, on the other hand, avoided being taken in by anyone. I had, during the next fifteen years, worked unknown with the humane society, which was against the maltreatment of those of the animal species. I instinctive found homes where the owners kept and mistreated all those they had taken in, the majority were feline. The thing I would always do when I located such horrendous conditions had been to bark outside of the home of the nearby neighbor at midnight. I would then run to the abuser's home, causing the responding officer to follow me in an effort to capture me, but when they were about to lay hands on me, the stench from the home would cause them to alert the SPCA. By morning, a judge would sign the order to enter the home. Fifty-six cats and seven bodies were taken out. The fifty-six were in dire condition.

As a reward, I received several pats on the head from appreciative firemen and policemen. My crusade was to rescue as many as I could mistreated animals. My guess is I covered four states. Then as all things must come to an end, my last discovery was of a house containing forty ill-treated felines. My reward was the usual pat on the head in appreciation for what I had done.

The fact that one of the policemen had taken me to his home was almost as great a reward that I felt for all the years I had helped saving those of the animal kingdom. I wouldn't have allowed myself to go with the policemen had it been months early as my time as yet expired. But I was well aware that I would breathe my last breath in two hours. I was too old to continue my crusade. I had been fed with the promise I would bathe in the morning and be taken to the veterinary, but none of that was to be.

POLICE K-9
K-9 POLICE
LICE K-9 POL
K-9 UN
K-9
K-9

I licked his face several times in gratitude. All was silent. Content, I closed my eyes, and in an instant of time, I was transformed into the heavenly animal kingdom.

"Welcome back, Wag," said Bow-Wow. His words were followed by the thunder of applause from all in the great hall. Now that I was back and my memory restored, knowing why Bow-Wow had sent me to earth as protector, I believe that I had earned the right to again be appointed comforter. To my delight, Bow-Wow agreed. There were shouts of joy for my reinstatement as comforter.

Bow-Wow then suggested I join many others in our kingdom that were playing with the children that continually came from the adjoining heavenly kingdom. The boys and girls rode on the backs of lion, tigers, elephants, camels, zebras, and horses. Also, they would fly on the backs of eagles.

They all enjoyed the abundance of fruits. One of the favorite chosen was not grown on earth. It was called go-go. The taste of it was like an apple and peach. No one could describe its succulent juice.

Oh yes, it has been asked in earthly song if reindeer really know how to fly. The answer is yes! I am, at this very moment, looking at six reindeer and six children riding on their backs. All things are possible in this animal heavenly kingdom, and unlike the world, there is no end.

Bow-Wow, at this very moment, has sent several others to act as protectors. I asked Bow-Wow, “Why are you not sending more?”

He replied, “To save all the maltreated four-legged creatures wasn’t meant to be, as there is a lesson to be learned by those of the human race that commit the abuse, but all the mistreated shall be with us and live happy ever after.

The happiness expressed in the story as related by Wag in the heavenly animal kingdom can also be achieved on earth. As an example, those that give their allegiance to the current administration, not understanding they are being deceived and are enriching the leader of the party, comfortable in their ignorance and support. They refuse to acknowledge the facts contrary to their misguided belief. The fact is, they are giving an imitation of having a functional brain.

Printed in the United States
By Bookmasters